CRITTERLAND ADVENTURES

Dale the Whale

Story and pictures by Bob Reese

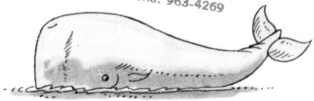

 CHILDRENS PRESS, CHICAGO

MY 35 WORDS ARE:

Dale	the	bed
went	say	can
swimming	will	breathe
in	get	I
Snorkel	stuck	anyway
Bay	but	rose
where	water	swam
little	fell	off
ocean	around	to
critters	head	this
play	got	day
no	oyster	

Library of Congress Cataloging in Publication Data
Reese, Bob.
  Dale the Whale.
  (Crltterland adventures)
  Summary: Dale the whale finds himself stuck in
Snorkle Bay when the tide goes out.
  [1. Whales—Fiction. 2. Stories in rhyme] I. Title.
II. Series.
PZ8.3.R255Da 1983   [E]   82-23588
ISBN 0-516-02313-6   AACR2

Dale went swimming
in Snorkel Bay

where "little" ocean
critters play.

"No! No! Dale,"

the "little" critters say,

"Dale will get stuck

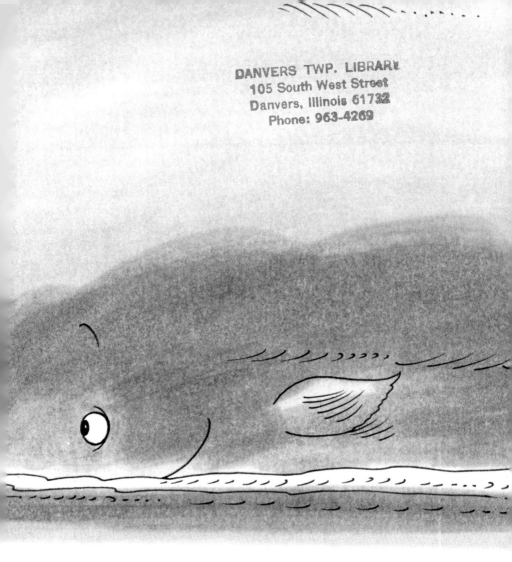

in Snorkel Bay."

But, Dale went swimming
in Snorkel Bay,

where the "little"
ocean critters play.

The water fell
around Dale's head.

Dale got stuck
in the oyster's bed.

"I can breathe
in anyway.

I can snorkel
in Snorkel Bay."

The water rose

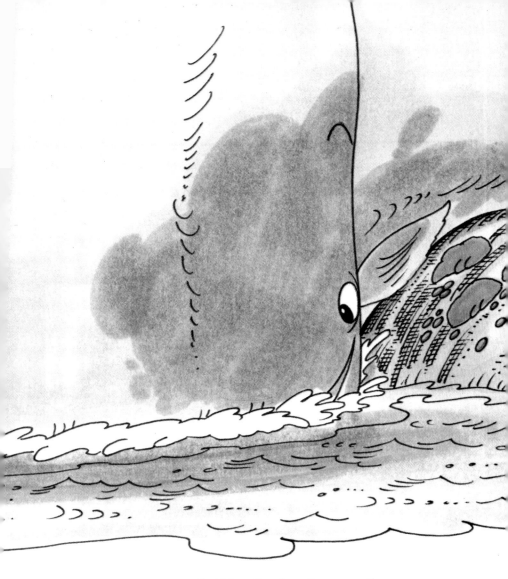

around Dale's head.

Dale swam off

the oyster's bed.

To this day,

"little" critters say,

"Dale got stuck

in Snorkel Bay."

Bob Reese was born in 1938 in Hollywood, California. His mother Isabelle was an English teacher in the Los Angeles City Schools.

After his graduation from high school he went to work for Walt Disney Studios as an animation cartoonist. He received his B.S. degree in Art and Business and began work as a freelance illustrator and designer.

He currently resides in the mountains of Utah with his wife Nancy and daughters Natalie and Brittany.